SUHRITA DAS

BLUEROSE PUBLISHERS
India | U.K.

Copyright © Suhrita Das 2024

All rights reserved by author. No part of this publication may be reproduced, stored in a retrieval system or transmitted in any form or by any means, electronic, mechanical, photocopying, recording or otherwise, without the prior permission of the author. Although every precaution has been taken to verify the accuracy of the information contained herein, the publisher assumes no responsibility for any errors or omissions. No liability is assumed for damages that may result from the use of information contained within.

BlueRose Publishers takes no responsibility for any damages, losses, or liabilities that may arise from the use or misuse of the information, products, or services provided in this publication.

For permissions requests or inquiries regarding this publication, please contact:

BLUEROSE PUBLISHERS
www.BlueRoseONE.com
info@bluerosepublishers.com
+91 8882 898 898
+4407342408967

ISBN: 978-93-5989-877-3

Cover design: Rishav Rai
Typesetting: Rohit

First Edition: February 2024

INTRODUCTION

***

Amidst research for unique subjects to develop screenplays, I came across the stories of gangsters in India. It was upon further digging into the subject that I found the unique story of Jena Baai, who was the first lady gangster. While I found Jena Baai's story to be very compatible with a large fictional work, there was very little information on her. Not only did she survive the most difficult shortages and crises in the country, but she was also a support system for a huge community. For a single mother who started her filmmaking career late in life (though 38 is not late at all), the legend of Jena Baai feels like a true inspiration for me. Obsessed with wanting to capture her long and illustrious life in fiction, I started writing Heera. This is my first book, and it covers one-fourth of her entire journey.

1

***

It is 1942, and the Students Movement to Free India from the British Raj is in its fullest fury. Dawn breaks in Dhonekhali, a remote corner of East Bengal (present-day Bangladesh). A woman in her 30s, Fatima, wakes up in her mud hut to stare at her children sleeping on thin beds spread on the dry, earthen floor. To her surprise, she finds there are only five of them; the section at the end is crumpled and vacant. Curious to locate her sixth one, she calls out, "Heera? Koi geli re Maa?" (Where are you, dear one?) She waits for a response. There's no sound emitting from any section of her hut. She gets up and gathers her 'abroo' (cloth piece that covers her like a screen), loosely wrapping it around her worn-out saree. Fatima peers into her husband's room.

Fatima's husband, Abdur Haq, is a senior professor at Dhaka University. His books and notes lay strewn on his study desk as he left it two months ago when he last left home. A large photograph of Gandhi adorns his wall, and a metal crucifix and a little Radha Krishna picture hang beside a framed Alif from the Koran. Fatimaa cleans these every day when she enters his room, breathing hard to still find his smell—the stiff, bitter essence of his tobacco—lingering in the air. Nothing comes to her but memories. She then puts a cross with a pencil on the calendar hanging on the wall, marking another day gone without his return. Finding her young girl missing here as well, Fatima goes to the kitchen, thinking she might have started the earthen cooking pit to make tea for her mother.

But the empty kitchen stares back at Fatima. She growls under her breath for Heera, who must be in some part of the village helping an elder steal vegetables from the nearby farm or plucking tart berries from someone's tree who might be still sleeping. As Fatima sits on a wooden stool and starts the fire to make herself tea, she notices grains of rice and lentils strewn on the floor. She gets up promptly and begins looking into the large earthen pots. To her shock, they are all empty. Fatima has used every grain of rice and every dot of lentil meaningfully to stretch food to her six children till the end of the month. Most of the time, she has been stuffing her stomach with the starch water drained from the rice with a pinch of salt. Her head is now bursting with rage, imagining that Heera must have taken out everything to help another home in the village. Fatima now races out of the kitchen, calling out into the hut, the surrounding thicket, and the stretch of river flowing by. "Heera? Heera?? You nitwit of a girl, your father has spoilt you thick. Who do you think you are? Now come home and see what awaits you!" !!!!!

The curses and threats of Fatima echo and resonate in a thick forest that once used to be gardens and orchards belonging to the Nawab of Dhonekhaali. While the forest remains unpruned and densely filled with wild boars, hayenas, and jackals, it is said to be a hiding place for dacoits and, of late, the revolutionaries. In the middle of the forest, a dilapidated palace of the Nawab gapes at the sky, waiting endlessly.

It is in this forest that little Heera finds herself a walking path while balancing the sack of rice, lentils, and potatoes. A light crunching into the dry leaves covering the earth, and Heera cautiously stops in her tracks amidst the thick forest. She looks back, high and low, with no one there, and yet she feels someone is there—someone is walking with her. She recounts the ball of paper that came into their room in the darkness of the night. She woke up with a start and opened it in the silver haze of the moonlight leaking into their room. She recognised instantly her father's neat Bangla instructions and then, without wasting a second, followed every chore, not disturbing her five siblings and mother. She knew Abbu's faith in her, and this was the day when she was going to prove him right.

Just when Heera feels she is about half an hour away from her destination, her worst fears come alive. She almost can't believe her own eyes. The village money lender, Moni Laal, stands in front of her in his crisp white dhoti and kurta. A pen from England shines in his breast pocket. She doesn't know why he is here. Heera thinks of a way to escape this man—to turn away or do something. But he has come to take Heera away, not let her go. Two boys jump from behind to blindfold her eyes, pick her up, and race somewhere. Heera hasn't let the sack go; she holds on to it with her life while her agile, active mind ticks away. Has Moni Laal sided with the dacoits? Will he take her and sell her off in Calcutta to balance the long-due money of her Abbu? Will she ever see her parents and her five siblings again? After a while, Heera, feeling parched in her throat, begins to feel dizzy. She passes out, unable to hold her head high. She feels someone take away the sack from her, which she can't defend anymore.

Heera's eyes open after what feels to her like several hours. Her head feels light. There's only that much rice she had early last evening, and she feels a groaning pain in her head. The girl, all twelve, tries looking around only to realise she is sitting on a dusty floor. Its paining, sharp pains shriek from her back and her head. They must have slapped her and beaten her hard on the head again and again. Something feels moist under her nose. She moves her leaden hand to reach out and realises it's a stream of blood.

Upon looking up, she finds a distant figure looking at her. It's not Moni. It's a Gora Sahib. Seeing Heera stir, he whispers something to a constable beside him. The constable runs away to call back Moni. Moni races with anger and frustration in Heera's direction. Heera's body again shrivels up in fright. He holds her chin up with his cold, calloused hand and calls out, "Baap koi tor? Deshdrohi kahaa kaar!!" Where the hell is your father? (He is a terrorist.) Little Heera's mind blanks out; it is only now that things begin to make sense to her. Something tells her they could finish her here, in the middle of nowhere, but that's not how she will end. She nods innocently at Moni and calls out, "Jaani naa (I don't know).

Moni slaps her bruised cheek and repeats her words in a mocking tone. This is when Gora Sahib gets up from his high chair and comes up to where Moni and Heera are. Heera notices the wooden cane in his hand, the revolver secured around his waist, and his blue-shining eyes. They are cold, but the man gently bends down to look at Heera closely. He holds the child with his hands and picks her up. As she shivers, he slaps Moni in the face. "What is wrong with you, Moni Lal? This is a child! Look at what you have done to her." Moni, who so far knew that the sole purpose of picking up the child was to find out the whereabouts of her father, cannot connect General Leuten's changed perspective towards her. He mumbles under the thunder of the slap, still reverberating on his cheek. Leuten continues with Heera, "You are not to worry, my child, not an inch, not a bit. Sorry about this that he has done to you. You can go."

Heera can't believe her own ears. Is this what a true British officer is like? She is reminded of the heated arguments her father and his friends used to have about the students bringing news to her father about them peeling off nails and skin to extract information. This must be a kind officer, then. She will tell Abbu about him, she decides while eyeing the confused Moni.

He calls out to a constable standing close by, "Eh, bastaa laao!" (Bring her sack.) The constable obeys and brings the sack. Heera is reassured to see that nothing has fallen off it. She smiles with cheer. She gets up on her feet to take the sack, and then, bending to say a sort of thank you without wasting any further time, walks away. The child walks as fast as her thin feet can take her, the weight of the sack and her own reeling head pulling her down.

As the day rolls into the evening, Fatimaa again borrows a little rice and lentils to at least cook one meal for her children. Her children play and fight at a distance; the one who kept them together has gone, and tomorrow she stares at them, uncertain and darker. As her heart feels an unknown fear, wondering why Heera isn't back yet, Fatimaa wonders whether to sell off the hut in portions or her last gold bangle. She holds close the chit Heera must have tucked under her pillow before she left. Abdur's handwriting makes Fatima's heart cry out. She stares at the river from a distance. As she sets up the earthen pyre, much to her discomfort, she lets the paper ball into the hot fangs and watches it burn. She sets up the water on a large pan to cook, knowing he is there; he will come; their child by now must have reached him.

Heera walks into the thicket, the light showing her the path and saying it's close to evening. She knows the forest like the back of her hand, having been here since her younger days with her Abbu. At nightfall, she knows the snakes that will slither by and the bats that will hang over her head. But she will reach the dilapidated palace before daylight wipes it off completely. An angered Moni, in his broken English, tries to ask Leuten: What is it that he did wrong? Why did he slap Moni in front of the child? The tall, broad Englishman smiles with an evil glint in his blue eyes. He calls out, "It was necessary, my dear. So what if you were slapped? Here's your reward!" Leuten takes out a thick bundle of currencies and tucks it into Moni's palm. The shrewd money lender, for whom every minute of life is divided between profit and loss, finds it incomprehensible and wonders why Leuten is doing this to him. Without wasting much time, the British officer now calls out to his task force, "Follow her." A smile now surfaces on Moni's face as he finally gets the plan.

A lot of time has passed as Heera walks slowly through the forest. She sings to herself the soft lullaby her Abbu used to sing to her and her siblings. A song of a fierce princess standing in the face of danger guarding her clan, a song of determination and rage, while the world has lost its centre, a young princess brings order. Ever since he has gone into hiding with his students, she sings to her siblings and puts them to sleep. Heera is the closest to her Abbu, and today she will prove he can trust her with anything.

Sundown is not very far, as the birds chirp back home and the air feels lighter and cooler. Finally, after trudging for what must have been almost another hour, Heera finally sees the dilapidated palace peeping out at her. The last leg of reaching out seems like an impossible task, but she pushes herself hardest and finally enters the dusty, broken architecture. Her Abbu has told her the tale of the coup and the King's descent into madness. Nothing lasts, he had told her—no king's glory, no kingdom—even the Britishers wouldn't last for long; they would give up and leave them to breathe in their own country.

Finally, in the darkness and amidst the buzz of the forest insects, Heera comes to the edge of the palace. She can see no stirrings, no feeling of life inside. She calls out with a whistle and waits. Still no sign of anybody. Cautiously, she looks back again to be sure there's not a life watching her. Again, she whistles, this time a gentle whistle, as if in response to her's, it's a reply from the dark palace. A smile lights up on Heera's face. She softly tiptoes into the ancient architecture with its insides mostly chewed up, the centre of the palace a large gaping hole staring at the night sky. Now safely inside the palace premise and aware of her father's protective breath in the vicinity, she calls out, "Abbu? Abbu? Abba Jaan!" Heera finally thrusts the heavy sack onto the dry, cracked floor. As she begins to wander here and there, images begin to lurk in the dark. She knows the bodies from their silhouettes. Her Abbu is tall and lithe in the middle, and on either side are his favourite students, Abdul, Razzak, Robi, and Torun. They gently walk up to Heera, and her Abbu holds out his hands to embrace her.

As the father and daughter meet after months, Heera feels her father's embrace weakened and his arms thinner. His eyes moisten as he holds his closest child to his chest. "Heera amar buker dhon (closest to my soul), my spoilt one..the only one who knows what I really set out for." In the semi-lucent moonlight, as Professor Haq feels the dusty yet firm face of his daughter, he senses a trail that has dried and caked under her nose. It sets his senses alarmed immediately. "What happened to you, Heera? Did the police catch you and beat you? Did they come home to ask for me? Are you.." Heera shooshes a much-agitated Abdur to say, "It was Moni Laal. He slapped me and asked where you were; he even took me to a white officer; I did not say a thing, Abbu."

At this point, the boys exchange a glance and look anxiously at the wide, open entrance of the palace. Haq, still numbed by the sensation and much-needed comfort of finally getting to meet his daughter, pays less heed to the truth of her freshly coming away from having met a British officer. He holds the child close to him. Heera asks him, caught in his spindly arms, "Why was Moni calling you a terrorist, Abbu? Is it wrong to fight for freedom? Will these white people ever leave?" Haq looks Heera in the eye to explain, "It is our birth right to be free, my child, and you have just fought with us by not telling them anything. Remember this forever: one girl can do more than what hundreds of boys can do. Will you remember that? And freedom fighters are heroes, not terrorists." The girl, overjoyed with what she's just learned from her Abbu, gets up and goes to fetch her sack so they can all quickly boil a little rice, lentils, and potatoes together. The boys signal that they should all move to the upper quarter, where there's a room where they cook whatever they can get—wild roots and berries—and sleep on haystacks spread on the rough, cold floor.

But when Heera comes near the sack, her heart trembles as tall shadows walk towards her. It's the Goraa sahib, Moni Laal, and two of his constables. General Leuten has a glint of evil on his face as he matches eyes with Heera. Heera knows what's about to come. She turns to warn Abbu, who is still waiting for her to bring the sack. But even before she can call out, the sound of bullets pierces the air. The boys come racing to Haq, and in seconds, they all lie piled on each other. Five of them, who were alive with smiling faces and burning eyes a few minutes ago, now lie still with bullets all over their bodies. The rice and daal lay blood splattered on the floor as Heera rushes to her Abbu.

She wails in the dark night, "Abbu, Abbu!" if she could only save him from the bullets. But it's all too late. His bullet-infused body lies beneath the bodies of two of his boys, all sixteen and eighteen. The Goraa's laughter fills the air. Heera wails above his vulgar laughter, unable to comprehend what just took place. Did she just get Abbu killed? Heera holds Abbu close to her face, and Shalwar Kameez drenches in his blood. Will she ever go back to a place called home? What will she tell her mother, who waits for him? She got him killed!

Moni is bewildered by this sudden showdown by the British officer, who had promised that he would arrest Haq and his students. But this is what he actually wanted—to finish them here and erase their very existence. Moni calls out to ask why he shot them, and the officer continues to laugh as his constables drag the bodies out of the lost palace. He then looks at Heera. Moni has been a senior; he has envied Haq and his family; he has seen Heera being born. Ashamed of having led the officer into this for a few extra rupees was enough for a lifetime to recover from. Just when he senses the officer is going to snatch Heera for himself, Moni lets out a yell and holds her. Moni guards the little girl, knowing her fate—being defiled by the officer and then being thrown away into a brothel in Calcutta. The officer takes it easy. He says, "Calm down, Moni; I need to clean away these bodies first; only then will I take care of her." Heera knows exactly what is being told.

Night rolls into dawn. The sound of the earth being dug at a distance can be heard. Leuten walks up to Heera and says, "If you act smart, I will kill you too and bury you here with your father. You hear that?" Heera breathes hard; something has snapped in her; her tears have dried. She remembers again and again that she will never get to see her Abbu again, that the country is yet to be free, and that a girl alone can do what a hundred men can do.

At dawn, a large and deep grave is dug. And as the golden rays of the sun hit the earth, five bodies were immersed in the womb of the earth. Nobody will know of their existence; their contribution to the freedom struggle will never be documented, and Leuten will have shed another trouble off his back, making it easier for himself to get to the next trophy, the land promised to him. Moni stands, holding Heera close to him. The moment the last lump of earth is put on the grave, Leuten turns to Moni. He shows a thick stack of notes; this will be enough for him to take it and leave the girl back. But Moni shakes his head, holds Heera close, and tries to slowly walk away. As soon as he is a few steps away, the same bullets fire in the air. Moni, now scared, lets go of Heera's hand and runs away into the thicket, yelling, "Run, Heera, if you can, girl, or this is your end.".

Leuten leaps forward to hold Heera by her hand while the constables have hurt Moni in his foot. As Leuten begins to drag Heera away, she uses all her might and force to stop him. Unable to deal with his energy and knowing the inevitable awaiting her, she eyes a sickle glistening near a heap of crops kept close by. Even before Leuten can pre-empt what's about to unfold, Heera bites into his hand. He, unable to bear the sharp pain, lets out a yell and lets go of her hand in a split second. She races to the sickle, and even before the constable, or Leuten, can lay his hands on her, she digs it into his chest.

Her body is bursting with fierce anger and sheer helplessness at watching her father die before her eyes; she is unable to comprehend life beyond this minute. Heera continues to dig—the girl who studied and did her sums right in class, the girl whose father wanted her to stand tall and make a name for herself in the world. Heera, the only older sister her younger brothers and sisters looked up to and whom her mother confided in, was unable to stop herself from butchering a British officer. At a distance, the mail train passes by, carrying muslin and yards and yards of cloth and matireal to Bombay. A part of her says she will have to leave as soon as possible. The constables, in no time, will gather their forces and comb the forest to get at her. Now they will not wait to rape her but kill her straight. She picks up the sickle, rubs off the blood to hook it onto the dupatta, which she has now wound and tied around her waist, and races to get to the mail train. Wherever she goes, the world is somehow fatherless.

There is no need to be good, correct, and true in her father's eyes! He lies buried under thick earth. Heera, sitting huddled amidst rolls of muslin, cotton, and khadder, sings his lullaby, looking out at the distant rising song.

After hours of sitting huddled and staring out of the distant door, bringing in the draft, Heera finally arrives at the large and bustling Victoria Terminus. She had heard about its structure from her Abbu; she knew she had reached Bombay City. Heera slips out of the goods train before the labourers can roll out the goods. She crosses the rail tracks and finds people in hoards moving in a direction. She follows them.

Having followed the crowd, she emerges from the station premises feeling tired and hungry. The thought of doing some odd job, which might not be unusual in a large city, crosses her mind. She begins looking for small shops to do some cooking, cleaning or scrubbing their large burnt pots and pans, and at least have a meal. She comes to a shop where she pleads and manages to clean tables and wash utensils at the busy shop that sells curries and bread. Many other boys and girls of her age and older than her work with her. A distant radio plays a silky male voice lilting, "Heaven, I am in heaven, and my heart beats so that I can hardly speak." from some distant land. The customers eat and leave; time turns.

At days end, when they sit in a row and eat on their steel plates, she tries and asks a coworker here or the cooks if they know someone or a group working for the freedom movement and if she can participate in the sloganeering or rallies. But no one knows anything. Only occasionally, when the parties emerge singing songs and bullets fire in the air, Heera is revisited by her night at the palace, and she passes out in fear. A large part of the year passes by.

In her sleep, lying on the red cement floor of the shop, she dreams of their hut in Noakhaali. Her mother must have started selling their land to stay afloat. Moni must have died in the forest, and Fatima must be thinking Heera ran away too with Abdur. But Moni escaped that evening, despite being hurt in his left foot by the bullets. He wailed and sought forgiveness from Fatima. The villagers shoed him until he breathed his last. Fatima stayed awake all night staring at her children and making a plan to sell the hut for some money, but at dawn she went to Abdur's room, locked herself in, and hung herself with her Abroo.

With the oppressive and humid heat waves of the bay turning into monsoons, Heera wakes up to a new reality. The incessant rains keep pelting on the roofs, streets, and lanes. Collecting in every nook and cranny, it just keeps raining and raining for three months. The little corner in the food stall they allowed her to sleep in has to be packed and rolled in to stop water from clogging inside. Heera finds it impossible to find herself a place to sleep at night and come back for work the next morning. She begins walking again, in the rain, drenched and soaked, her tears melting away in the flow. She sings to herself quietly the lullaby of her Abbu. "O princess who lives in lost lands, your dreams of your own make you fly; no one asked where you were sailing, and yet you sail. Sail, O princess, one day this unknowing will take you to your known land.".

Heera keeps walking for hours in the rain, surviving on the chapattis she had last packed from the food stall, which are now soggy and inedible. Her head reels in high fever. She has come to the end of her tether and knows she will drop on the road and pass out when, at a distance, she sees the tall spire of a Kali temple. Its black stone walls and high, sharp spire call out to her. A silken red flag hoisted on the spire magically flutters in the wind despite the lashes of the rain, as if giving a sense of direction to the directionless. She walks up to the fluttering.

All Heera can see is a stretched-out, thick tarpaulin shade near its front door. The roads are empty, and the lanes are deserted. Even the freedom fighters singing 'Vande Mataram' while walking in rows have taken shelter in another corner. Heera feels like the corner on the cement staircase is only calling out to her. She races in its direction and slides under the black, glistening tarpaulin. She hears someone call out to her with open hands. It feels as if, at this moment inside her fevered head, someone just spoke. Someone tells her, "Heera, your father might not be there in the world anymore, but there's us, this city, and its people; the world has a corner to it, and this is yours." She doesn't know if someone truly said those things to her, but the minute Heera steps into its realm, a warm pair of hands seem to embrace her and put her at peace. She falls asleep on the cement floor, protected for once from the continuous sheets of cold rain.

Heera has lost count of the hours she slept, but at dawn, the aged patriarchal priest of the temple, Tailang Thakur, who cleans and sprinkles holy water on all corners of the temple, is shattered to see a sparkling Heera lying crumpled in a corner. He tries pushing the girl awake, but he notices her body is burning with fever and her lips murmur a few words only: "Abbu I killed you. I killed you, Abbu." Tailang, the seasoned devotee of Goddess Kaali, knows the goddess has brought one of her own to his door. Though in high fever and rambling in her sleep, Tailang's eyes don't miss the rare, sharp, and divine face of Heera, as if etched out by an artist with great care and attention. He feels it is his duty to take care of the child. She was waiting to be seen by him.

Heera opens her eyes in the middle of the night on a tiny wooden bed. Tailang sits at a distance, praying to the goddess. He has laid out a spread of freshly cut fruits and sweet meat before the goddess, and he himself is chanting from an old scripture set up on a wooden stand. Oil lamps burn. The smell of camphor, the burning lamps, the glistening red tongue of the goddess, her eyes, and shimmering gold jewels play havoc with Heera's brain. She calls aloud for help. Tailang picks himself up from the chanting and comes to attend to the girl whom he has attended to and laid down on his own thin, hard bed. Seeing Tailang in his 'Kapalik' attire of a red tilak on his forehead and a black dhoti with strings of rudraksh hanging down his neck, Heera gets further terrified. She calls again, "Abbu, don't kill my Abbu. Don't; he will free us; he will free the country." Even before Tailang can say a word or reach out to the earthen pot of water to sprinkle some water on her face, the girl passes out again.

After three days and two nights of continuous delirium, throwing up whatever Tailang fed her, Heera finally finds the strength to sit up. Tailang sits at a distance, looking deep into her eyes. As she sips the hot drink, he has made her boil with spices and herbs. Tailang asks, "Eh, little girl, you certainly have run away from somewhere. Where do you want to go? What did you do? Do you have blood on your hands? I have allowed you into my Maa's temple; she is also an angry woman and drinks blood. Tell me? And what is in that tiny bundle you guard under your head all the time?" Heera silently stares at Tailang, wondering if he will understand the truth. But her silence irritates Tailang, who is determined to find out where she has come from. He insists, "You killed someone?" Heera gently nods her head and confirms.

Knowing her fate of being thrown out, she keeps the drink aside, stands up, and takes out her bundle. It's her sickle, which she neatly keeps bound by her weathered dupatta and carries with herself like an organ in her body. As the instrument glistens in the room, looking straight into his eyes, she says, "I killed the British officer who killed my father." Tailang is struck by the girl's ability to stay unwavering with the truth. He asks, "Where?" Heera calls out fearlessly, "near the Dhaaka border, on the Dhonekhaali side. Please don't get me arrested; I have to work for the freedom of this country; my Abbu left his task unfinished; now I must do it." Even before Heera finishes her words, Tailang steps forward and slaps her across the face, leaving a deep, red trail on her tender skin. "Now that you've told me about your Abbu, promise that you will never again tell this to anyone. You can stay here with me, clean and care for the temple, work with me and my boys, and see what I do. But tell your truth to no one. Only if you promise this, will I let you stay here?" Heera tries to plead,

"But the country and its freedom?" Tailang now asks her, piercing her with his gaze, "Did they kill your Abbu or not? So do you want to die or stay alive?" Heera's eyes brim as she is freshly revisited by that oppressive night when her Abbu let out Vande Mataramonce and for or all. She nods to Tailang in agreement with whatever he says. Signalling at his goddess, he says, "Like she holds on to her khaada (sword), don't let go of that sickle of yours; it's your third eye that will tell you before time what's to be done." It is from this moment that she knows her life has changed in a seamless city, amidst a sea of unknown faces. It is a miracle that her heart is still beating against her chest, and she has found another voice, another tall figure who, almost like her father tells her, says that before anything else, it is most important for her to stay alive.

Weeks pass by as Heera slowly recovers from the trauma of her past and adapts to her new life. At 4 in the morning, Heera wakes up even before Tailang has stirred. She bathes and cleans the temple floor, and she washes the metal lamps and utensils needed for Devi's worship. Then she goes to the market and brings the choicest fruits and flowers when Tailang finishes his bath and starts the worship. The day goes by distributing flowers and Prasad to the worshippers of the Devi. They come from various religions and castes. Devi's temple was established in the 18th. century by a clan of robbers who claimed to have dreamt of her asking for her temple to be established and prayed to. It is said that she is alive and awake. She listens to her children and fulfils their wishes.

After the evening Aarti, Tailang sets the Devi to rest and locks the main door of the temple. The young boys from the neighbourhood await him at the back door, from where they head in the direction of the dock. Heera follows them and does as told, not making a sound or asking a question. They wait patiently, hidden behind large boulders, watching the bay glisten in gold and silver. As they silently wait, almost stopping their breathing, Heera, staring at the bay, travels in her head to her hut in Dhonekhaali, wondering what her brothers and sisters must be doing and what she is doing. Mother must be looking like now. Before tears can brim in her eyes, she quickly returns to the present.

After hours of waiting and when sleep is almost pounding on Heera's eyes, they hear the distant sound of the steamer. The boys eye each other, and Tailang, covered in a long black gown, tiptoes towards the shore. After a few minutes, he emerges with wooden boxes on his head. The boys help him bring the boxes down, and he brings back more. Before the first rays of sun hit the shore, the boxes are moved away from the shoreline to a distant abandoned go-down. As Heera waits with the boys, a few burly men come and take charge of the boxes, giving Tailang a few crisp notes. He salutes them, signals the boys, and goes into the day distributing money to each of them while keeping a stack to himself, which in due course he will give anyone who comes to Devi's feet and pleads for a little financial respite.

One week, one month, and one year go by. Heera knows that while the whole country is ablaze with rejecting foreign goods and commodities, what comes in those wooden boxes are items from foreign lands that the rich and aristocrats use inside their guarded mansions. One day, unable to stop herself, Heera finally asks Tailang, "You pray to Devi, offer her everything, and vouch for a life of purity. And yet you smuggle in foreign goods into the country and make some money? Why? Does your Devi approve of this?" Tailang smiles at the child. He gently holds her face and says, "Do I keep the money to myself, Heera?" The girl nods in agreement. Tailang then explains to her, "If you do something wrong that does greater good to others, you must always do that. Only do that, Heera, the Devi understands. Don't you see her? With a mighty sword, she is herself out to kill the damned and draw blood from a crazy world." Heera stares at Tailang and wonders what it means to do good for a greater good.

Late that night, Heera wakes up Tailang. She sits at his feet and says, "I will do what it takes to do a greater good, Baba. I will." Tailang barks at the sleepy child and says, "For now, do yourself some good by sleeping. Rest; when your time comes, you will know. The Devi sets up each one for his or her work."

3

***

Four years have passed by. It is 1947, the 15th. Day of August. The country is free, and its air is bustling from all corners with the reverberations of "Azaadi." "We are free; India is a free country."

Telang, a little bent and weak now and blind, sits on a charpoi in the middle of the Dongri slum. The temple bells of the Devi and the Azaan at the town square mosque ring aloud in the August air. People are gathered from all ends. Workers, labourers, women, and children sing and dance, sprinkling gulaal of pink, red, and green colours at each other. The radio is turned on in a nearby tea and bun maskaa stall. There is hope for a new world, though lines have formed and borders have been laid across hearts and lands. Heera, a seventeen-year-old brimming with youth and fervour, lives in the heart of the slum. As they cheer and smear Gulaal on each other, a man in his fifties comes racing through the crowd, calling out to her.

This is her fifty-two-year-old husband, Tabrez Alam. With youth growing on her and himself getting frail in his eye sight and might, Tailang found it risky to let the girl be by herself or have only the temple premises as her home. Left to herself, she had split her life between the temple hours and sloganeering at the party office. She needed to belong and be what she was: a woman. Tabrez, a widower with two sons, Rizwaan, seven years old, and Haider, five years old, needed someone to run his home, take care of his food and clothing, and be there when he would be back from his long business journeys. Tailang found this to be a suitable proposal for Heera, and much to her dislike, she got her married.

Tailang can gauge from Tabrez's walk that he is not the happiest of men to see his wife melt away in the united revelry of the country's independence. Even before the old man can get up and warn her, Tabrez gets hold of Heera. He catches her by her hair and slaps her. This sudden act brings the revelry to a shocking silence. To them, Tabrez is all that Heera has projected before them. A well-meaning, orthodox, reserved man and a dutiful husband. But to Heera, this isn't new. His sudden violent attacks, unpredictable mood swings, and the abuses and pains he hurls at her are not unknown to her and the two boys, who find Heera to be dependable, someone they can confide in as they would in a mother or an older sister.

The boys come running to take Heera's side. The slum has been silenced. A raging Tailang comes tearing at Tabrez, seeing this. But even before the old priest can say a word, Tabrez raises his hand and warns him, "This is my house, and she is my wife; stay out of it, Pandit. Enough!" Tabrez holds Heera in his iron fist and calls out, "I told you to make us chapaatis and tie up our things; we have a night train to catch. We are going to our country, our land, Pakistan. What happened to that? Do you care to give me an explanation or not?" As Tabrez continues to slap Heera, she wails out, "But this is our country, Tabrez; this is where we must live. I don't want to go anywhere, no other place; I will die if I leave my country." Heera's suggestion makes Tabrez lose his temper completely; he goes berserk and beats Heera black and blue for the next half an hour. Anyone who has come to stop him or protect Heera has had no choice but to get away from Tabrez's range. Heera takes the beating like a seasoned creature, and then, with one final blow, Tabrez finally throws Heera on the dusty earth with blood gushing out of her mouth. The raw taste of blood and the grainy taste of the loose earth in Heera's mouth make a smile appear despite hot, warm tears of humiliation rolling down her cheeks. Before Tabrez can lay his hand on her one last time and drag her away, she pulls out her sickle from inside her kameez and, with great effort, stands up to reach out for Tabrez's neck. A scared Tabrez, never having seen his wife in this avatar or with this instrument, steps back.

Heera smiles gently through her tears. "My Abbu has given blood for the independence of this country, Tabrez. He might not be on the list of freedom fighters, but that doesn't mean it's not true. Now this country is mine, and I won't give away what is mine. Go away or I will cut off your head right now, failing which I will slit my own throat." Heera's eyes have the possession of the goddess she has served these past few years; it is clear that she will execute what she is saying. Tailang, aware of the girl being possessed by the raw, bare energy he had seen in her the first day she came to the temple, walks up to her. He looks at her, awed, in teary eyes, and in joined hands, pleads aloud, "The Goddess showed herself; my years of prayers have not gone unheard; she has shown herself in you." The crowd cries out the name of the goddess.

A cornered Tabrez now rightfully looks around for help as he is facing a mad woman, with the temple priest making it worse. But to his surprise, bit by bit, the crowd now gathers on Heera's side. Rizwaan and Haider hold Heera together. As the threat occurs to him for the first time that his sons might abandon him too, Tabrez calls out, "Rizwaan, Haider, let's go; the train will leave in two hours; we will go away to our much-promised land of milk and honey and live a new life. Come away; this is a 'chudhail' (a witch); she has done 'kaala jadoo (black magic) on you two. Rizwaan, all of seventeen, speaks up for himself and his brother: "Heera is our Maa; you go and live your life in Pakistan; we will live with our Maa." Tabrez lets out an unearthly laughter upon hearing this. He calls out, "Maa? My foot. It takes a man to earn a living, run a home, and take care of its wellbeing. Where will she feed you two from? By selling that dried-up body of hers? Well, there won't be any takers. You will die of hunger or become thieves; come away!" Heera now stops an infuriated Rizwaan from further engaging with his father. She calls out, "What a hundred men can do, one woman can do Tabrez. I will take care of my boys; now leave or I will throw my sickle, and it will only rest after claiming your head."

As the sickle glistens in the sun, Tabrez, without wasting another second, races away. The crowd gathers to nurse Heera, and the boys get her water and wipe away the dust and blood.

As they cheer for her courage, Heera's heart beats aloud in fear, glaring back at her like a thousand wild hyenas. She has studied a little Bangla and Urdu at home and some Hindu scriptures from Tailang, but the new jobs are calling for education while those set up in mills and factories are being thrown out. She knows there's only a few hundred rupees stacked away in a lozenge tin in her kitchen rack, a pair of gold bangles Tailang had given her on her wedding, and the three tiered neck laces and waist band that Tabrez endowed on her and had sex with her every night, only urging from her womb a son, another boy. But by the time they go back, Tabrez must have sucked out everything and left. She wonders how she will run her life and live along with that of her boys. They are both studying in a school run by the nuns; they eat well, wear freshly embroidered kurtas and thick leather mojris (slippers), and their comfort is in a house whose rent comes every month from Tabrez's trade. Now who and what will take care of their needs? Heera silences her mind and tells herself, "One day at a time!"

Late at night, Heera wakes up feeling hot and unwell. As she worries if she must have eaten something that went wrong, she gets up, unable to stop herself from puking. She throws up the little chapatti she had chewed at night, breathing hard and wide awake. Heera knows she is pregnant.

4

***

The days are slow, and the nights are slower. Two years have passed by. Heera has been a gentle, caring mother to the boys and her little girl, Panna. By now, bit by bit, Heera has sold her bangles and necklaces until it has come down to the last thick gold band that Tabrez had tied around her waist the night before independence. It now feels not like an ornament made of gold but like iron fetters he had put on her to keep her trapped in its lust. Rizwaan and Haider are both in school, but they keep failing. Panna is yet to wake up to the world, but Heera wants her to study. If Heera can pull it off for another three months, then chances are that she will get a job in a flour mill; they are starting close by. The rent will get higher nonetheless, as will the cost of sugar, rice, and cooking oil. Heera stares into the dark night and wonders what happens after this. They will be out on the roads, and she will be responsible for the boys going astray and her daughter being snatched away from her. The thought makes her breathless.

One morning, while the boys are still sleeping and Panna is sucking at her breast, Heera has the final act of courage to visit her. She beats the thoughts and worries shrieking in her head like the howl of a thousand wolves with a definite and absolute action. She gets up after the infant has gone back to sleep, takes a sharp plier, and breaks off the waist band. She wraps it in a dupatta and holds it close to set off for the local jeweller, Parikh. While she feels lighter without the ornament tying her down, her heart pounds heavier, knowing it's her last asset.

Parikh, sitting in his shop with iron grills separating him from the customers for whom stools have been placed outside, takes a closer look at Heera. As she bends down and pushes in the scarf, his calloused hand brushes against her soft, fair Heenaed fingers. He has touched her other jewels earlier and seen a flash of her, but something tells him this is the last one. They always come with one last item, and that's how Parikh knows their backs are against the wall. For women whose husbands have been drinking or have been thrown out of jobs, Parikh has a reputation for being a deal-maker. Heera knows all that and yet.

He touches the thick metal and gauges its worth and weight, but his strokes seem like he was trying to derive the warmth of Heera's body from the cold, lifeless ornament.

He looks at her, then looks back at it. Heera looks away, asking coldly, "Kitna dega Parikh? Jaldi kar" How much for this Parikh? (Make it quick.) Parikh picks up his steel cup lying beside him and takes a long sip of the thick, brown tea, then thoughtfully comments, "The market is down now, and Tabrez is also not there to bring you money, I know. I can suggest something by which you could keep the ornament as well as have some money. There are three mouths to feed. What you need is regular money, am I right?" Heera looks back, glaring at the aged jeweller. She feels angry and humiliated, but deep within she sits defeated, knowing selling this one piece won't be enough. She remains quiet, letting her silence do the speaking. Parikh gently slides the ornament back to Heera and whispers, "The mills, factories, and offices are stuffed with young men wanting jobs; no one will give you a job." Heera looks at him helplessly, knowing he is not lying. He continues while holding out a stack of currencies, "And if you work as a nanny in the big bunglows, they will pay you only for the baysitting, not the other job the employer will do with you in the staff quarter. So?" Heera is still there, with her back against the wall. Parikh says flatly, "Nine p.m., back door of my shop. I will be waiting; wear this and come; it belongs only to you." Heera hears every word, quickly takes the ornament, wraps it back in her dupatta, and races back home.

The boys will not be up yet. Panna might be up but will be playing with the wooden spatula and rolling pin Heera has left beside. Heera feels the thick roll of money in her hand and stares at the distant meat shop on the high road. It is a rare day, and she is tempted to make some meat for the boys and herself.

As the butcher strikes on the pieces of meat she has selected, Heera feels it impacting her body. As if she were now cutting herself up into pieces to offer bit by bit. All for a single cause: "I will not leave; this is my country!" She takes the meat wrapped in a newspaper, shouting out the perennial unemployment of the country, the rich getting richer, and those in the middle being thrown down to poverty. When Heera comes back home, as she had preempted, the boys are still sleeping, with one of them running a fever. Panna crawls up to her and kisses her on the cheek. She sets up the sauce pan for a cup of tea as her hands and feet feel cold.

As the water boils, the vapour rises. Heera stares at it and wonders how and where her day will end. She just confirmed to the aged, infamous Parikh that she would offer herself to him and that he would give her money in return. The day rolls by with the boys going out to play, eating a late lunch of the goat curry that Heera has cooked with the money Parikh gave her, and rice. They wonder where the money came from for a feast; she scolds them and asks them to focus on the eating. She whispers, "Ghar ki baatein bahar mat bol, chupchap khaana khaa. Mat pooch kahaa se aaya." (What happens at home stays at home; eat and don't ask for its source.) In the late evening, Rizwaan's fever comes down, and Haider sets out to go see a local fair play. He carries their baby sister along. The house, with a fevered Rizwaan in a corner, shrieks back at Heera. As night deepens and people get back to their rooms early for the week ahead, Heera's head throbs and her chest beats with a fear of the unknown. The act is the same: Tabrez used to pull her late at night and force himself on her, but now she is willing herself to do it. With a stranger. The act will define her. She bathes, clips up the waist band back on her waist, hangs her sickle onto it, and wears her clothes. Rizwaan, who is still weak from fever, questions Heera as she steps out, "Kahaa chali Heera? So jaa." (Where are you off to now, Heera?)? Go sleep.) Heera looks back and gently says, "I will sleep when it's time; the mother sleeps last, Rizu. Keep a watch on Haider and Panna when they are back."

The streets are deserted, and Heera walks with each footstep, feeling as heavy as lead. When she enters the lane of the market, she sees a few stray dogs standing in a corner fighting over raw bones the butcher must have thrown at them. They gnarl and fight, and Heera is scared one of them might pounce on her at any moment. She silently crosses them and finally comes to the back door of Parikh. She gently taps on the tin door. There's no response at first, and then the door opens automatically. Heera stares at the dark vacuum, staring at her. At this moment, as she walks into the darkness, she remembers the earth being dug by Leuten and his men to drop her father's body and the young boys one by one. The earth ate them up. The country was finally free, and India, Pakistan, and East Bengal were formed. People settled within the borders, religions, jobs, and things to do. But everything blurs in her head. What stares at her is the next day, another week, and so many years of bringing up her children. Nothing matters anymore—nothing but the sleep, rest, clothing, and feeding of her children.

Heera enters a dark room with a thin and long lamp flame at one end. The darkness will chew her up and spit out her old idea of herself tonight. She has come to submit to it; let it flush her out on the other side. She wants to know what lies there, where they say she should not step in. A thin slice of bed with a white bed sheet on it is visible. Parikh sits on it. He has removed his brocade jacket. For the first time, Heera sees his face more clearly. When she sees him closely, she realises there are no ill names written on his face, and his eyes glitter with the childish exuberance of waiting to open a new toy. Heera gently removes her dupatta and begins to remove her kameez. As she bares herself in the light of the lamp, Parikh stares at her fair skin and the gentle rises and falls of her body with the adoration of a devotee. The gold waistband shines, and her sickle hangs from it. Heera gently removes the sickle and places it by the lamp. She then offers herself on his bed, having crossed over to the other side. As the older man devours her body for an hour like a famished beggar, Heera tells herself, This is what the prostitutes must be feeling like every night in the brothels in town. Touched, but not touched at all. In a single moment, she becomes one with them, travels an untraveled journey, and finds herself as one of them, not looking down anymore.

For the first time, Heera touches her own silence. It has been following her without her acknowledging it so far; it is a silence where she cannot share her pains with the ageing, blind Tailang, her noisy neighbours, or the young boys who think she is their mother. No one is in that silence with her. She is the mistress, the queen, and the decision-maker of her fate. With her eyes, she sees a tomorrow that no one else can or ever will. As Parikh draws pleasure from entering Heera vigorously, not asking her but telling her when to go under, above, or beside him, she softly sings to herself the lullaby of her father. Of a fearless princess who rode alone the tide of time and stood to stand and protect her community.

Towards the edge of dawn, Heera requests that Parikh let her go. He dismantles her, pulls out a thick bundle of notes, and offers them to Heera. As Heera picks up her sickle, puts on her clothes, and readies to leave, he asks, "Tomorrow, a friend of mine will join us after me. I have told him yes." Heera turns and stares at him speechless, defeated, aware that it's not the mountain peak she has climbed but just a few feet above ground level, "the money will be double." She nods obediently, tucks the money in her fair breast, and walks out into the dank air, calculating her things to do. Something has shed light on Heera; she is lighter from the burden of being nice and correct. She looks at the distant horizon as the sun rises. No one will know about her, and no one will bother to find out what food her children ate or what clothes they will wear. She alone will have to make sure the wheels of the home keep running. With the horizon lighting up, something broadens and brightens in Heera. Boundaries, lines, and differences in boxes of name, religion, and creed disappear. All that looms is a need. There is a need for a mother to bring food and a little extra money for her children, even for whom she is actually not a mother. But Heera won't stop at that; after her home has had enough, she stretches out to the home beside, and the one beside that, tucking in an extra note into the hands of the women. A greater good she now feels the achievement of.

The tryst with Parikh and his other male friend went on for about a year. Heera was silent and made a great catch. The money kept them going; the neighbouring women took small loans. Their sudden needs for money being taken care of by Heera made them wonder what was going on. She kept telling them it was the jewels; she was still grateful to

Tabrez for having left her such an asset, while it was her body and the blood and hunger for survival flowing through it that made her travel each night. Parikh had rented a room for her in a shanty at a distance. One night, when he didn't feel up to it, he sat back and watched Heera offer herself to his people. He said she would never have to look back; she could go on until her children would grow and make a place for their own income. Parikh even kept the Thanedaars in his pocket, allowing them to enter Heera's room once a month. Just when Heera was thinking that despite the oddity of her job and the risk of getting into an unwanted pregnancy, it gave her security, one night she crawled up to the room to find it locked and Parikh missing. Her heart thumped as she pleaded that things were alright.

Parikh had died. In his home, he suddenly fell and breathed his last. And with that came to an end the neat, clear arrangement that Heera had managed for about a year to keep her kitchen pyres running, fresh clothes on her children, medicines if they fell sick, and school fees.

All over the country, there was unemployment staring back. Parikh's monks would see her through another two months at the most, after which running her home would become impossible. Tabrez's words hit Heera hard every single day, but what stuck on was her Abbu's words. What a hundred men can do, a woman can do. When push came to shove, she offered her body and brought money. Then why was she falling short of anything at all? She could go to the tall buildings on Peddar Road and ask for work. Cooking, cleaning. There were still Gora sahibs living in the country with their families running companies. She could be looking over their children or cooking for them. Perhaps they would not spare her after that, but she wasn't shy with her body any more, like a coy housewife. She knew why men left back their wives and came to the other. The other was the wilderness—a lure, a promise. A part of Heera now resisted it; Leuten's face never left her. She saw him in each of them and wanted to go for a kill.

As she stays wide awake late at night, thinking of what to do, she steps out and begins walking aimlessly. In the darkness, in the lowest of her beings, there is a voice that never left her, that threw her back into life no matter how cut away she felt from it. Her feet take her back to the Kaali temple. They had covered its cement sitting area with stone slabs. She sits on the cold stone slab in the hot night. Sleep comes by. In the depths of the night, the temple's back door makes a noise. Heera wakes up with a start. She tightens her chest and slides into the temple, feeling the cold surface of her sickle against her warm belly. As she sees a stooping, dark figure walk by, she is almost ready to make a swift swing at the shadow when she realises it was a withered Tailang going for his night rendezvous, with his sharp instincts for what is there. His eyes almost lost visibility, but sharp ears and measured steps kept him on the turf. She comes and stands in his way. As the depth of the night is interrupted by the chirping of the insects and occasional dog howls, Heera falls at Tailang's feet. She pleads, "Baba, you gave me life; now help me and my children stay alive. Teach me what you do, and I will do it better. I cannot become a maid servant in people's homes. I am too proud of that. And I can't ask you for money either. I have traded with my body, but I don't feel like a sinner. But now I am back to staring at nothing. Show me a path; I promise you I will bring more, much more, for everyone to share. Let me earn it." Tailang feels Heera's moist eyes, his own eyes streaming with tears, hearing about how she earned money for a year. He sees the girl with his mind's eyes, knowing she has a rare spirit. She is extraordinary. Her spark cannot be contained in the frame of a wife or a nobody. She is meant to be one of her kind.

Feeling that rare pride shine through her, Tailang says, "Fine, then don't do this feat alone; call your boys. Let them go with you; they must earn their roti, and all you must give me is a hundred rupees. I need to support the families of Manoj and Razak in our slum; they have gone jobless this week." Heera nods. She understands beyond what is told.

5

***

Since 1954, rice has become rare and expensive in the country. Every home and every quarter of society needs it and is paying a price, whatever price, to acquire it.

The most astounding jobs or lucrative offers in the world are all about responsibility. This is what Heera wakes up to later that night as she and Rizwaan stand with a hand cart inside a large cloth mill, waiting to download more sacks of rice to be taken away and stocked from the dock.

Across rolls and rolls of cloth at one end come muffled sounds. A sturdy, large man is pulling down thick sacks of rice from a hidden loft. As Heera and Rizwaan stand closeby with Tailang's hand-pulled cart, the man keeps piling the thick rice sacks. After a while, he stops. Heera stares at the cart, then begins counting in her mind. She stops at something then calls out, "Eh, throw in some more!"

Rizwaan calls out from the other end of the cart, "Heera, you are out of your mind? We will be able to push only this much." Heera glares at the boy and sooshes him. "You get lost; I will pull away everything on my own. Did you count how little we will make if we pull only this many sacks?" She now growls at the man, "What are you waiting for? Throw in at least five more sacks." After a little while, when the sacks are neatly placed, Rizwaan piles up a lot of scrap aluminium and copper sheets to conceal them. They start their onward journey. The task is enormous; to Heera, it seems like she has taken the whole of the earth on her back. But after a few steps, she starts breathing out and setting up a rhythm with Rizwaan pushing the cart from the back. They slowly leave the lane of the mill and come to the cross section, where they should have taken the left as the police station is on the right.

As Heera moves the trajectory of the cart towards the right, Rizwaan, scared, calls out, "Heera, you are going wrong. This is the way to the police station; they will catch us in a second." Heera places her finger on her lips and signals Rizwaan to shut up. The narrow, dark lane, which they avoided as safe, is where police constables were hiding in civil clothes. Heera had heard from Tailang about excessive scrutiny and checking, with the rice ban now reaching its peak. They stagger through the lane they cut across the police station. Heera notices the chief officer standing near the verandah, supervising the lane on both ends. As Heera enters the lane, she begins abusing an imaginary man for not taking responsibility for his family. Rizwaan, confused, continues to push without asking any more questions. They cross the police station and take the rice sacks from right beneath the nose of the police officer, who is least of all able to gauge what could be in the cart. The possibility of a woman pulling away a cart full of scrap could be capable of participating in the most banal crime of the time, rice smuggling.

They finally come to the handlers of the ill-reputed Prasad Seth. They have been dealing with the aged, blind Tailang for years, giving him his usual two hundred rupees and taking away the item at scarcity at the moment. They are taken aback to see a young woman carry the load forward with a nine-year-old lad. Heera, seeing them, calls out to Rizwaan, "Rizu, count the sacks and tell them our rate." Rizwaan, aware of these handlers of Seth and himself, a scared boy, calls out meekly, "Ten sacks—two hundred each. You pay us two thousand rupees." The handlers almost didn't hear at first, but upon hearing Rizwaan quote the price, they burst out laughing. "Two thousand? In your worst nightmares, have you seen two thousand rupees? Here are your two hundred rupees; get the sacks off." With this Narayan, the first handler throws the notes at Rizwaan and then suddenly takes out a gun and holds it on Rizwaan's forehead. A shivering Rizwaan begins taking the sack when Heera flashes her sickle on the second handler, Javed. "Here, you touch my son, and I slash the neck of your friend." Javed, who can feel the cold blade of the sickle on his neck, has almost stopped breathing. But what he does not lose sight of are the fierce eyes of Heera in the pitch-dark night. There is something he sees in them that he has seen in someone else. He calls out, "Narayan, enough is enough; we know how much Seth makes out of each of these sacks; give her the money, take the sacks, and let go." Narayan, unable to carry on the truce any further and left with no choice, throws the balance of the money at Heera, then signals them to leave. Rizwaan exchanges a look with Heera, and the next thing they know is that they have won the first battle of power.

Heera comes back to Tailang and gives him all the money at first. Excited with her achievement, she says, "Pandit, this is my first one; there will be many, many more after this; you don't worry, you can keep all of this." Tailang sees the stack, slowly counts his two hundred rupees, and returns the rest to Heera. He says, "You do what you want with the money, Heera. I need only two hundred dollars to help the two boys who lost their jobs." Heera stares at the balance of eighteen hundred rupees in disbelief, though she is the one who has negotiated it. She has for the first time earned after her nights with Parikh, and it will be enough to run the next few months as well as feed everyone in the slum on Diwali night. She kisses the money and tucks it away in her blouse. She whispers to herself, "What a hundred men can do, one woman can do. A woman can do anything."

This is the first Diwali when the slum comes alive fully. Heera has asked Rizwaan and Haider to arrange for food for everyone. If khichdi is what they can manage, so be it, and there are clay lamps in every house. They put large Dhaaks together. After years of listening to the dhaak beats, in her village in Dhonekhaali, the October sky used to be filled with these beats, welcoming Goddess Durga for five days. At nine in the night, after all have cleaned and set up their homes with clay diyas, rangoli, and hung kandils, they come to gather in the centre of the slum. The ageless banyan tree stands calling out. The two jobless boys have received their money, and Heera has distributed a little for each home, knowing she will bring more and fetch for them all.

The boys sing and dance in cheer. Tailang sits on his rock at the banyan tree, watching Heera emerge from a girl to a woman, from helpless to helpful.

But the handlers who left with the rice sacks paying an unheard amount of two thousand rupees had it coming for themselves from the Seth. He could not believe they let a woman leave with two thousand rupees. He knew he could charge extra for the fine, long-grained basmati, which was scarce all over. There were homes in the city that would pay anything to acquire it, but old Tailang, who has been doing this job for the past few years, seems to have dug his own grave by handing over the task to a woman. That too, someone who commands her price. Seth sees this unseen woman as a potential danger. He calls out to them, "Kill Tailang Pandit; just pick him up and get him killed. It shouldn't come to me, but the message should reach that bitch. This is not her place for doing things, and this is most certainly not how she can get things going." They nod to his instructions and leave. But while one plans to talk it out well to Samarth, the police officer of the area, the other, Javed, leaves in the opposite direction. Javed is the one who felt the edge of Heera's sickle on his throat.

He races in the direction of Peddar Road for the old stone building of Jalaal Seikh. Seth gives him work and money, but only that much. For long, Javed has been wanting to enter the circle of Jalaal, who has all the illegal trade going on in the docks, markets, and airports. Jalaal pays his handlers sufficiently well too, but there are very few boys he works with. He is choosy, trusts no one, and has issues with people who seem too steeped in impressing him. Jalaal is arch rivals with Prasad Seth. Javed schemes that if he can bring this woman into Jalaal's fold, then Javed can have a punch and a leap in his income.

Late at night, Jalaal sits on his terrace and watches his young boys take aim and practice with guns. Three boys, aged seven, three, and five, play with guns and pretend to be taking each other's lives. Their mother, the ripe and overflowing Nazneen, with her flowing brown hair and reeking of a thick itr (perfume), comes chasing them while keeping an eye on Jalaal, whom she has been fiercely attached to from a very tender age.

Jalaal watches the sun go down while aged faqir Peerzaada Sahib recites poems from Ghalibnaama to him. Jalaal listens to them with attention. Asks him to repeat anything that touches him deeply. He notices Javed in a corner. Jalaal has picked up the pulse of a person more than anything else. It is said that he is almost a soothsayer in the trade. Javed's presence tells him that he brings some news that Jalaal must hear. He asks the senior Peerzaada to pause for a while, rest, and take a sip of water while he calls Javed to himself. Javed bows and honours Jalaal and then whispers in his ear. Jalaal listens with full attention, then thinks for a while. Jalaal is never mistaken about an action, and he is what he is owing to his promptness. He looks at the horizon and then gives Javed a nod.

Back at the slum, excitement is reaching its peak with the poor people gathered for a song and dance. They bring Heera to the centre to join them. Theirs cheer and a sense of well-being after long. Javed enters the crowd and eyes Heera. Heera, who knows from a distance that Javed has come with a purpose, excuses herself and comes away towards him. His news brings nervous anticipation to Heera. Her heart skips a beat for reasons unknown. She tries to say she will come with Javed another day, but when she looks at the dance and cheer, she wants this party to carry on; she wants to keep bringing them money. She calls out to Rizwaan, whom she can trust completely, and explains, "Bacha I have to go and meet this Jalaal Seikh. He wants to see me." The name Jalaal brings an unknown fear to the young Rizwaan. He says, "Heera, you can't do this alone; I am coming with you. He is dangerous; his temper is more famous than his achievements." Heera passes the boy and says, "Now we will have to decide who does what. If we have opened a shop, we must allocate responsibilities. You and Haider take charge of the night; look out for Panna; everyone must eat; and have mithai. Even if extra people come, no one must go without eating. You two take care of this community; we have to be there for them while I go meet this sheikh and see what he wants from us. Goh." Without wasting another second, Heera turns away and melts into the dark with Javed, while Rizwaan returns to the people of the slum.

At two in the morning, Javed brings Heera to Jalaal's fortress. The high, impenetrable walls of Jalaal's prophecy enclose his concealed world. It is the world's most notorious and smart smuggler, Jalaal Sheikh. Javed continues to whisper to Heera, "You must bow and wish him heartily. Keep your head bowed. And don't say no to anything he offers—any work, any money. He is stuck with huge rice stalks, unable to cross the ports. He is not a Chindi chor; he is a dil daryaa. If you ask for two, he gives ten; that's why there is always so much work he has. Understood?" Heera hears everything, but a part of her refuses to accept something. She called out, "But why must I bow my head? Is he Allah or Maa Kaali? My head bows only to my Allah and at Kaali Maa's feet, and you know that." Javed, remembering he has quite a mess at hand, sooshes her and says, "Okay, then at least be quiet. Remember, we are all wanting to work with him; now you have to make that possible."

After waiting for ten minutes in what seems like a huge living room, they are finally shown the way to the staircase. Heera feels she sees someone looking at her from across a thick curtain of coloured glass and wooden beads. A strong and thick perfume haunts her. Her senses are unmatchable; there is no mistaking that. And she knows it is a woman— a woman wearing a perfume wanting to mark her territory. After a while, she withdraws, but Heera continues to feel her gaze on her. When they climb the stairs, Heera asks Javed, "Is Sheikh married?" Javed looks back uninterested and replies, "Three sons he has; I think he has a grandson too." Heera asks again, "How old does that make him?" Javed stops in his tracks and replies with an assured gaze, "Ageless! I don't know if he was always around and always at the top of the heap. But it's getting tough for him to do it by himself now." They flush out onto the terrace. It is cool this late at night, with the saline sea breeze blowing in and making a gentle sound amongst the pots and plants lined around the terrace. No one can see from the wide street below what's going on up above. They sit on wooden benches kept at a distance from an elegant arm chair, which must be Jalaal's seat of control. A telephone sits beside it, as does a paan daan. There are a few books kept on a tool in a heap close by that must be very old—all in Urdu, ageless poems, and Nazms. A string of jasmine flowers coiled up above it.

Heera suddenly feels her heart tremble. She grasps Javed's hand and whispers, "Javed, hume kaatke dariya mein phenk diya to? Mere baccho aur bastiwaalon ka kyaa?" What if he chops us and throws us in the bay? What happens to my children? And my slum? Javed now looks at Heera and says, "You are a gem; I saw it in you the first time you bargained with us. He knows what he is getting! Just know that you are not what you deserve, but what you negotiate. This saudaa (deal) can make or break you." Within the next few seconds, a couple of young men come up and stand near the large chair. A tall man in a Pathaan suit emerges from the staircase. There is a strange silence in the air and a vastness. A vastness of someone having arrived. Heera is struck by the silence in her chest. After he has settled, one of his boys comes up to talk to Javed. They whisper amongst themselves, after which Javed tells Heera that Jalaal will meet her alone; he will wait for her outside the building.

Even before Heera can protest, Javed leaves with his two boys. A few minutes of absolute silence persist. And then his bare, thick voice crackles in the air. "yahaa aiye." (Come up.) Heera hesitantly gets up. He is invisible to her, just a large form with a shawl loosely hanging around his body. In the beam of light, she can see the loose end of his shawl on the floor. Heera gets up, her body suddenly feeling as light as the wind. It feels like an invisible force is drawing her towards this dark figure sitting still. He isn't doing anything, and yet he is doing it all. He is playing her; for the first time in her life, it feels to Heera like even if she tries to resist him or walk away, she can't go beyond this point. She stands closer to him now, still not sure which seat to occupy. He raises his hand and signals towards a tool exactly opposite him.

It is now that Heera notices a tiny lamp flickering near it. She sits down, fearing she will fall on the stone floor. Her body shivers with an unknown excitement; she wasn't aware of this kind of vibration inside her until now. Her breath races, and she finds the silence unbearable. Heera tries to see Jalaal's face in the darkness, but only gets a glimpse of him. After a few minutes, his voice crackles again: "Aapko yahaa bulaaya kuch baat karne ke liye, magar baat humse hon nahi paa rahi hai. Yuhi beythe rahe?" While I wanted to have a word with you, I found it difficult to speak. (Should we sit like this?) Heera sits still and nods. It feels like anything he asks for, tells her, or directs her to do is fine. She will be fine sitting thus. The night passes by as they sit opposite each other. Jalaal nurses a tall glass of whisky kept near him. He then says, "Bohot raaton se soye nahi hai. Hum aankh band kar lenge toh aap chali toh nahi jaayengi?" (I haven't slept for nights; if I rest a little, will you leave?) Heera nods in a nod, though an unknown urgency tells her she must get up and walk away.

The minutes pass one by one, and the sky turns pale. It is only in the fading light of dawn that Heera sees Jalaal for the first time. As he sleeps like a child, she can't find any trace of a ruthless criminal in him. His sharp, tall nose, bare forehead, and the kurta exposing his chest make her feel magnetically drawn to him. This is when she notices a huge scar on his chest and one on his forehead. Her hand rises to want to almost touch them, but Heera feels she must leave beyond this point or else she will loose her own strings, with which she holds back herself so hard. Her feet feel like lead. Heera gently comes up to Jalaal, pulls his shawl to cover his chest, and walks away as gently as she can.

Javed waits opposite the building, sitting on a high rock. As soon as Heera emerges, he catches up with her. On her way back, Javed asks her a lot of questions, but the fierce woman he left with Jalaal Seikh in the night is not the one coming back. She calmly reports, "Aaj baat nahi ho paai" (today no words were exchanged between us). When they come near the slum, she says, "Jhoote hai, unhe koi baat karni hi nahi thi, iss tarha mera waqt mat barbaad kar." (He lied to you; there's nothing he has to say; don't waste my time.) Saying this, she walks away into the slum.

6

...

When Heera comes back to the slum, while she is hoping they have had their bursting of crackers and full feast and must be resting, she finds a haunting silence and the entire slum gathered. Rizwaan, knowing Heera even from a distance, races towards her. "Heera kahaa thi raat bhar?" (Where were you all night?) Heera asks, "Why did this happen? Didn't I arrange everything and go? Panna is alright."As they walk into the silent group, she realises it's not the little girl; something more grave, far more serious, has happened. Her eyes miss Tailang, who usually steps forward as an unnamed leader from amidst them. She calls out, "Pandit? Where is he?" Haider now calls out, "The police came and searched his quarters in the temple. They threw out some larger bundles of money, which couldn't have been his. They took him away to the police chowki." This sets fire to Heera's consciousness. She asks everyone around, "Why are you all here then? Waiting for what? You all should not have allowed them to take him away; you'll have followed and gone to the police station by now." Their silence speaks. Without her, they are rudderless now; they have no voice, no will, and no sense of direction.

An angered Heera races to the police station, calling out for Samarth, the haughty police officer. The slum dwellers follow her clues with torches in their hands. But once at the police station, the hawalders block the entrance, allowing none of them to enter. Heera throws herself into an open fight with them, matched by Rizwaan and Haider on either side. When a ruckus has taken a large proportion, a junior officer comes out to call out, "Who is Heera amongst you all?" The ruckus stops, and Heera identifies herself. "Only you come." The officer turns to go inside, and the hawaldars allow Heera to enter. Heera looks around and above to make a note and keep track of where she is being led. Though her eyes are fierce and raging, her heart is thumping aloud with an animal fear of being beaten or attacked at any moment. The tall building, with its arches and open windows, is cool. Within a few seconds, Heera is taken in front of a row of cells, where they keep suspects overnight before releasing them or transporting them to jail.

She is brought in front of a tiny cell, and as the officer opens its thick door, she is struck by the thick smell of stale urine. What stares back at Heera is Tailang on the cold floor, staring at her with his cold, stone-still eyes. His mouth had guzzled, and his body had leapt for a fight, it seems. His body is still lying stiff, like cold meat inside a refrigerator. Heera almost finds it difficult to breathe for a few seconds. Then, after a while, when she can sense the air and her own beating heart, she lets out an unearthly cry.

For three days and three nights, Heera sits guard at the Kaali temple. She doesn't let its lamp go off for a second. In the middle of the night, when the slum is sleeping, she weeps alone, not letting them hear her cry. She weeps and calls out to the only father she had after she ran away from Dhaka. She cannot let go of the memory of his cold, still eyes. He must have called for help; they must have strangulated him. Truths are not told, but arrived at. It is anything but a natural death, as they claim; her hungry, thirsty mind, alert and awake, tells her that.

At the end of three days and three nights, Heera gets up and finishes the last rites of Telang, letting his ashes flow into the ocean. She comes back to drink a gulp of water and chew a chapatti. Calmly, she asks Rizwaan, "Who did it and why?" Rizwaan sees the flaming rage in Heera's eyes, and he is scared she will do something they will have no return from. He stutters, tries, and looks away. "We asked for too much money from Prasad Seth; he got us Heera. He got Pandit, and thus got us. You can't cross swords with Seth. He got Samarth to do this. We are helpless people; we can't command our price if we are to be in this business."

Heera holds Rizwaan's face with her iron grip to emphasise, "You can only and only survive by commanding who you are, Rizu. Otherwise, they will trample us." Haider comes to join them, and he is nervous that Heera, their only protector, will take adverse action. He growls, "So? What will you do now, Heera? Go and slit Samarth's throat. Will you keep slitting the whole world's throat with your sickle?" Heera glares back at Haider and calmly replies, "Yes, I will. If need be, I will slit the throat of the whole world, but this is my dhandaa, and I will do it." Rizwaan, scared, calls out, "You are a woman, Heera. Who all will you cross swords with? They will get us even before we start." Heera, now done and settled in her mind, gets up. Looking at the goddess and bowing before her, she whispers to herself, "What a hundred men can do, one woman can."

Jalaal stares at the ocean out of his large villa. While the sea shimmers in the mid-day sun, his eyes look restless. He is looking for something he is unable to find. Javed stands close to him. He has brought the news of Pundit's death to the Dongri basti. The sudden accusation of theft and then death in the prison cell. Jalaal is curious to know where Heera has gone. Javed says, "She's gone, not in the busti; they say she is looking for the cop." Jalaal stares at the ocean, knowing for certain where she must be, as what he has seen in those eyes couldn't have been doing anything else. He whispers to Javed something that takes the young ruffian by surprise. But a command from Jalaal is what it is.

Like a hungry tigress, Heera keeps looking for the police officer. The cold eyes and stiff body of Pandit haunt her; they wouldn't let her rest or sleep. After two days of searching with Rizwaan and Haider by her sides like two little foot soldiers, she finally finds the corrupt police officer in a brothel. While Rizwaan thought she would draw him out and make him confess his crime, Heera has no time for any such thing. She pushes the large Pathaan pimp standing at the gate of the brothel and breaks into several doors until she finds Samarth in one of the rooms, oddly not with one of the girls but cutting a deal with one of the goons of Seth. She races into the room, holds him by his collar, and, looking into his drunk eyes, asks, "Why did you kill Pundit?" The police officer, drunk and with his hands stuffed with fresh currency, has no explanation to offer. He gently looks at Heera and replies, "Why should I give you an explanation, you slut?" This boils the blood in Rizwaan and Haider, standing close by. But before they can punch him, Heera takes out her sickle and, with one stroke, slits his throat, the blood springing on her face and his clothes. She stares at his cold, still eyes. The voices in her head seem to calm down slowly. Rizwaan takes the sickle from her hand, pulls her away, and they race out of the brothel from the back door before the Pathaan can find out and raise an alarm. Javed and his men reach the brothel late; he sees the slit in the throat of Samarth and knows the woman has come.

Rizwaan and Haider get Heera into a cart, and they come back to the slum. The boys are scared and angry. Rizwaan calls out, "You cannot keep doing this, Heera, slitting throats. Now that is a police officer, they will come sniffing for us." Heera calmly states, "Fear Rizwaan; they want us to fear them. If someone doesn't raise her sickle and reply, how will they know that they have reasons to fear too?" When they return to the slum, there is silence. Heera walks into the temple and rings the bell. She closes the doors and doesn't say a word. Sleep comes to her on the cold floor in front of the large statue of the goddess. The smells of molten lamps, flower sap, and a whiff of sandalwood put her to sleep. Late at night, she hears a lot of commotion. She gets up from the floor and is about to open the doors when she hears Rizwaan whisper near the door, "Don't you dare open the door, Heera. Just stay put. We are here guarding you."

The police force has come charging and is angry. The officers keep asking each of the slum dwellers, "Who killed our officer, Samarth? Tell us, or each of you will be taken away; we will arrest everyone for the murder of our senior. Who amongst you all did it?" All that echoes back is silence. The officers eye the young girls standing with their parents. One of them snatches out a young girl; he calls out, "She will be sold for the best price, and we will relish the money and later savour her for free in the brothel. What say? You still want to keep silent." There is tension in the faces of the slum dwellers, and the other girls begin to step back. But the fear is clear and evident in their bodies, and they begin to snatch the hands of the other young girls. Heera, who can hear it all, is bursting to come out and state that she did it; she killed Samarth because he killed Pundit. Because she wanted to send a clear message, the reply for cold-blooded murder is murder. But the door remains locked. When the police force is determined and turning away with five of the girls, an elderly woman steps forward and says, "Let me tell you who killed your officer, Samarth." The officers turn back, vulgarly excited that their ugly trick worked.

They call out, "Tell us then!" The old woman continues with fierce determination in her eyes, "We did; we all did. We all, who were one day at a time oppressed, wronged, and hopeless with his interventions, did it. We did it." The police officers remain silent. Speechless. The old woman continues, "When oppression reaches its peak, the body doesn't fear pain or death anymore. He took away our aged, saintly pundit; you expected us to stay quiet still?" Heera's eyes well up with tears, her chest bursting with pain, and she feels a strong emotional chord attached to each one of them. Something is growing in her chest that throbs and throbs and feels like it will burst if she doesn't let out a yell. A blob of love that has lost its boundaries and is bursting with tears, pain, and sorrow all in it together. Somewhere that night, in the closed temple, a mother is born in Heera, fulfilling the need to own every soul and every being that cries. As if the Pundit had climbed down to whisper it in her ears, "Don't quench the thirst and hunger of only your own children; quench everyone else's. Be the mother, for it is only the mother who protects. She who protects the child in her womb can protect the world."

The officers say for one last time, "Now you see what awaits you all. Great unity you all have, right? When it comes to the survival of each one of you, we will see where this unity goes. You just wait and watch." With this, the sounds of the large police jeeps leaving are heard. The large doors of the temple open from the outside. Heera walks out in her blood-caked saree as the slum waits for her. They come close to her to hold her hand, kiss her hands, and say, "Heera, you are ours; you belong to us."

When a defeated Javed comes to Jalaal that night, saying Samarth had already been killed by Heera before they could reach him, he slaps Javed, saying he had asked him to help the woman. A defeated Javed confesses, "She is too fast, too direct. How will we know she will slit Samarth's neck?" Jalaal knew the killing of Samarth was going to ease a lot of his stuck work; the ceased goods would be released, and he would make minimum losses. Jalaal knew his profits like the back of his hand. He then gently taps the face of Javed and asks for her to be brought once more. "Pichli

baar baat nahi ho paai, iss baar toh baat karni padegi."
(The last time I didn't have a word, this time I will.)

The woman who left that dawn from Jalaal's fort was not the woman who came back. It is not the same place where she has come back. Javed brings Heera, after a long journey, to a villa in Alibaugh. It seems like a kothi, an ancient haveli once full of people. The minute Heera steps into the building, her body is set alive, and the long, blunted pores are now open. She has not let her body respond for a long time to the attraction of others. But with Jalaal, she finds it impossible to stop herself. The inside is cool, and the floor beneath her feet is smooth.

Jalaal waits for her in the inner courtyard of the kothi. In the sunlight, for the first time, Heera looks at him. He looks different from the sleeping man at dawn; the scariness on his dark face is more evident than ever before. Something is scared inside Heera's, and yet something is fearless. A part of her wants to keep staring at him; a part wants to look away and run. Run away from her own desires, which she is feeling unbearable under the heat of the day and the heat of her own breath.

He signals her to sit on a chair opposite him. As soon as she sits, he pushes forward a bundle of currency and says, "This is your share." Heera is taken aback. "Share? What did I do to take this?" Jalaal stares at her eyes wide and asks questions, hiding love and running away from desire. He comes close to her and says, "You did, without knowing you did. Samarth was sitting on my occupied goods, and they would soon go away to Prasad Seth, but now I can extract them and also get good rates. Now do you understand what you have done for me?" Heera nods. She picks up the currency and begins counting. Jalaal takes out his paan daan and places it before her. Shy but tempted, she picks one and pushes it into her mouth. As she chews the bettle and the spices stuffed in its belly come alive, Heera wakes up to the woman in her, fully finding it irresistible to look away from Jalaal's eyes piercing into her being. "I can work more; I need more money, lots of money for my people." Jalaal smiles and says, 'Why else do you think I called you here? Can you be my associate? I have this kothi to offer you. Live here, work from here; your operations will be discreet, and the money is unimaginable. I just needed someone like you who is fierce and a woman. It makes things easier." Heera sees the perks that Jaalal is offering her. But she is infuriated with the idea of staying away from her slum, the dust, the sound, and the confusion. She gets up, dusting her hands off the money. "You mean you want an exclusive fuck girl and an agent cum handler too? Sorry." Heera is about to walk away, enraged. Jaalal holds her hand. "Iss baar nahi (this time I will not let you go). As Jalaal holds her hand close, Heera feels her body on fire, her desires getting the better of her, almost making her head woozy. As Jalaal pulls her to himself, Heera melts in his strong, agile arms. His body full of bullet marks and sword slashes embraces Heera; their smouldering bodies make love in the kothi all night, and at dawn, Jalaal sleeps curled up in her arms.

When the day breaks, they have still not broken out of the spell of their new-found love and lust. They know they will soon hunger for more and need only each other's company. Heera tells of her journey to Jalaal, from stabbing Leuten to giving away her body to Parikh and his men to pulling the rice and cutting her first deal. Jalaal is lost in it. He is a man of few words; his childhood and growing up are all written in the stabs and stitches of his body.

Heera then gets up to gather herself, tie up her hair, and look at herself in the mirror. Jalaal lies down, looking at her, calling out for her again. Heera thrashes him and says, "Now what happens to our work and all those we need to take care of?" Jalaal walks up to her to hold her in his arms and says, "Everything will be possible if we do it together. Why don't we?" Heera smiles, and Jalaal continues, "Stay here, take this house, be my wife, and bear me children. Heera, I have fallen for you. I fell for you that night when I saw you in the darkness for the first time. I will be incapable of taking care of my work without you. Let's do this together." Heera pushes herself away from Jalaal. "You mean you want me to be your mistress? Is that what you think I am? A woman to tuck away out of town who will give you children and wait for you? Keep waiting?" This is when there are loud bangs on the bedroom door. Javed shouts, "Heera uth gayi? Prasad Seth ne gundey bheje tere busti mein, sab ko gharon se nikal rahe. Wo busti jalaa denge. Jaldi chal!!" (Prasad Seth's goons are throwing the slum people out of their huts; come soon or they will set the slum on fire any minute.) Jalaal knows she will leap into the burning pyre only as a hungry, hurt tigress would. He tries to hold her.

Heera's breath has turned into fire. She quickly tucks in her saree, picks up her sickle, and hides it beneath her pallu. Then, looking back with moist eyes, she calls out to Jalaal, "Maybe this is our last time. If you want me so badly and want to really be with me, come to my slum, come and live with us, and be my husband. Let's see your love and need for me." Jalaal gets up to hold her close. "Heera, I don't know where my next breath or footstep will fall. The police are always on the hunt and want to pin me down. Know that I love you truly, and that is why, here, take this." He takes out his pistiol from under his kurta and hands it to her. "Kitno pe chuuri chalayegi? Ab bandook uthaa" (How many's throats will you keep slitting? (Now pick up the gun.) Heera stares at the pistol as he still holds her hand. Tears streamed down her eyes. Gathering herself and stiffening her hearing, she finally tucks in the pistol and walks away into the blazing day.

7

***

The well-spread-out slum of Dongri is blazing with fire, lashing out like the fangs of an evil monster. Whose kitchen fire broke out or kerosene jar fell is not the concern anymore. They knew they had locked horns with a formidable force, too high above their levels. Some kind of lashing was up their street; they, who lived on very little and hoped for even less, knew this. Women and children wail as they watch their walls crumble and curl down to ashes.

The fire is spreading at a rapid speed, with the oceanic winds lashing in from the dockside. Little Panna is guarded by Haider amidst the group that has gathered at a distance. Rizwaan throws out their few things from their room into the open. When Heera arrives, the elderly men and women come up to her; their silent faces say it all. As thick, dark fumes roll out into the air, Heera lets out an unearthly cry of rage and helplessness. She calls out for Rizwaan. The little boy doing much more than his age can allow him to do comes up and softly says, "Prasad Seth, kuch nahi bachega Heera." (It's the doing of Prasad Seth; he will spare nothing.) Heera, without waiting for a second, calls out, "Chal" (Lets go). But just when she is about to strike back on the enemy, she turns to see the hapless state of the wailing people watching the last of their assets melt into thick rolls of fire. She says, "Pehle ghar bachaana hai" (first we have to save whatever remains). Though it is an impossible task, Heera initiates the men and young boys of the slum to bring out water pipes lying near the docks. Tailang had shown her these assets on his multiple assignments to bring illegal goods from the dock. For two hours, they struggle to adjust the unused water pipes with the reservoir at the dock and douse the fire. By the time the last of the embers go out, it is dawn. The tired, defeated lot finally let out a sound of hurrah—a victory, though what they had lost was gone forever.

But there is no rest for Heera. She knows there are innumerable people who are homeless now and have lost every penny and every cloth to put on their backs. She will have to give them something. Rizwaan and a band of young girls and boys with thick sticks in their hands and the edges moulded with cloth dipped in kerosene set out with Heera. After walking for about half an hour, they come to the posh, desolate locality of Peddar Road. Heera calls out aloud,

"Seth?!! Prasad Seth?" All that echoes back to her is a resounding silence. After a while, she locates the tall apartment as Rizwaan shows it to her. Without waiting for another second, Heera marches into the building premises. They torch the sticks they are carrying. One of them breaks into the tall, thickly carved door, and as they enter, they bring down the artefacts, break the crystals, bash the spread-out furniture, and set the plush living space on fire. Within seconds, the whole place looks like a pyre setting up to go fully ablaze. Heera is fierce, her maddened eyes looking for Seth.

A woman emerges with a child in a fancy frock and her hair tied with a satin ribbon, pleading with them to leave. They are probably his wife and daughter. Heera's heart stirs seeing the child try and take guard behind her mother, but keeping herself undeterred, she takes out the pistol that Jalaal gave her. Rizwaan and the others are taken aback to see Heera holding a gun. The young boy blows out a whistle as they declare war. The woman, now trembling, quickly joins her hands and shows a corner. For the first time, Heera senses the power of the weapon she holds in her hand. She brings the nozzle to the corner where she's been shown and calls out, "Baahar" (come out). Prasad, a tall, thin man with his hair oiled and his face grisly, comes out like a slithering snake. He looks at Heera and gives her a wicked smile. She wonders why the weapon doesn't have the same impact. She mutters in anger, "Basti kyu jalaaya?

Mere Baba ko kyu marwaaya?" Why did you set fire to the slum? (Why did you get my father figure killed?)

Prasad continues to smile, only breaking into a vulgar laughter while emerging from the hiding place. He begins to tease Heera; he mocks her, "She got a new toy—a new toy to play with!! You bitch, a gun has to shoot too. Do you know that? Didn't your secret lover tell you that? Did he just fuck you and leave you with a gun?" Heera flinches, knowing that in this game and chase, everyone is keeping an eye on everyone. Prasad knows about her rendezvous with Jalaal. As he continues to get more and more obscene with his laughter, Heera quickly lets the rebuke slide off her skin; she knows he is trying to weaken her strength by humiliating her. It's not okay for a woman to be in a relationship when it's perfectly acceptable and aspirational to have as many women as he has tucked under his belt.

She strengthens her nerves and feels the ground beneath her feet. Heera is now visited by the cold, dead eyes of Tailang lying on the prison cell; she can hear the loud shrieks of the helpless slum people. While fire catches on bit by bit to the corners and edges of Seth's rooms, it races through her nerves and blood vessels too, almost making her want to burst from her skin. Just then, they hear distant police sirens. The neighbours are alarmed; the smell of burning is striking them alarmingly, and the flames from the house are now visible and reaching out. Rizwaan calls out, "Heera chal, isne police ko khabar de di hai, chal chal!!

(Let's go; this bastard has informed the police; let's run.) Moments of delay could mean the police coming and getting them, and yet Heera is still calm. She looks Seth in the eye, and then before her head can burst in rage, she pulls the trigger. The young boys stare at the tall figgure of Seth as it gently falls to the floor. His wife, who was watching this drama unfold, is horrified, but instead of feeling a release and being thankful for the end of Seth, she suddenly leaves the child and runs towards the balcony. Knowing what's about to happen, Heera holds the child and turns her towards herself, covering her eyes as Moni had guarded her at twelve, preventing her from seeing her father's body being dumped into the earth. The maddened woman leaps from the balcony, leaving only a thud sound on the hard ground below. The police vans have reached the premises. Sadanand is a new officer who has been brought in particularly to trace the crime around the dock area and the fast-growing crime hub. If he gets them, there's no seeing daylight in the open again. He is sworn to his duty, just as Heera is sworn to her need to protect and provide. Two equal wants are a problem; Seth was the least of her headaches.

Not wasting another second, Heera turns to leave. But she stops in her tracks, seeing the little girl whimpering as the house has become a furnace. She holds the girl by her hand and follows Rizwaan and the gang down the spiral staircase on the rear side of the building. Sadand reaches the floor but boils in rage as he stares at the sickle Heera has left back for him lying near the door.

Javed stands still by Jalaal as his cantankerous wife, Nazneen, continues to throw tantrums. She asks why Javed hasn't gotten her masalas yet from the ship arriving from Saudi Arabia, Heena and saffron from Kashmir, perfumes, and when cash will come. Her voice gets on Jalaal's nerves. "Aap under jaaiye, kaam ki baat ho rahi hai." (Go away; there's something important I am discussing.) The woman flares up as her husband snubs her. She growls back at him with an animal instinct stronger than words: "Mein jaanti hu aapke kaam ki baat. Wo chokri, galaa kaat ti hai, ab kyaa use ghar layenge?" (I know your work, that slasher girl; are you planning to bring her here?) Jalaal gives one look at her, then he looks at the far stretch of an ocean, the large fortress of a house he's built, the cars in a neat pile, and the peace and comfort he has brought to his wife and children from years and years of every illegal trade he could get himself involved in, slashing, getting beaten, and being marked all over his body and soul. He closes his eyes for a moment. Heera's smell visits him—a sweet smell that emanates from between her breasts. He looks at Javed and says, "Yahaa per nazar rakhna, mein jaa rahaa hu." (Keep an eye on this house; I am leaving.) Javed looks at Jalaal, stupefied. He wails, "Bhaai, you are not safe outside; it will take them." Jalaal picks up his thick, old book of Ghalibnaama and walks away into the rising sun with the gaze of the day on him. It is not the walk of a supreme gangster; it is the walk of a devotee drawn to his cause, his goddess.

The smouldering smell of burnt asbestos, canvas, and tarpaulin rips the air in Dongri. Heera returns with the young group and Prasad's child. They sit in the centre of the slum. She asks Haider to take the child into his fold, along with Panna, who, by now relieved to see her mother, rushes to her arms. Meanwhile, without wasting time, Rizwaan and his friends pull out boxes of cash and jewellery they have brought from Seth's house. They begin to assess the worth of things. Heera looks at them and smiles shamelessly. "Ghabra mat, sab haamre khoon paseene se hi jade huye hai. Baant de." Why are you shy? This is all made of our blood and sweat. Give them away. The helpless, distraught people now gather around her as she stands up and says, "We will build the slum again, we will live together, and we will not let anyone overpower us, ever. There's a new animal in their zoo, Inspector Sadanand. Just knowing it is enough, we are not powerless." Heera takes out her gun and shoots it in the air; they all shout out her name in cheer. "Heera, Heera, you are ours; you are the giver." She gently takes back the instrument, and before putting it back under her pallu, she touches its steel butt. On it is engraved his name in Arabic. She runs her finger on it, as she knows all that will keep them together is this instrument. The memory of the little time she had with him will dissolve while she continues to kill evil shamelessly by looking it in the eye with this. As her people get busy being given as much as their needs are, Heera turns away to go to the temple at a distance and rest. A car engine coming to a halt catches her attention.

As she looks out, she sees a vintage car come and stop close to her. After a few moments, Jalaal emerges in a white kurta and pajamas. Unarmed and unprotected, he leaves his hands out in the air and walks up to her. Her lips quiver, her heart skips a beat, and the woman in her is unable to keep herself within the boundaries. The slum dwellers and the young boys are stunned to see Jalaal Sheikh emerge and walk in. He calls out gently, "I am here now, in your slum, with your people. I need to serve you. From now on, I will serve you and your people. Will you marry me?" Heera stares at Jalaal, speechless, letting tears hit the rims of her eyes and flow.

THE END

...

Epilogue

* * *

It is 1968. Dawn finds a Heera of 38 waking up in a tiny section of her series of rooms in the South Bombay slum. Her section contains a cot, a shelf that has her Janamaaz rolled into it, a metal statue of Maa Kaali, her minimal clothes rolled in another corner, and on the wall, a large picture from about a decade ago. Jalaal, their son Ashfaq, Heera's other children Panna, Haider, and the apple of her eye Rizwaan, and Prasad Seth's daughter Roshni, whose responsibility Heera had taken from the day her mother plunged and died.

As Heera stares at the picture, she remembers the day as clearly as the present. Jalaal and she had made a lot of money in a recent tryst and gone to a small fisherman's town by the sea with the children. Heera raises her hand and, in the magic light of dawn, puts her finger on Jalaal's smiling face. Her senses come alive the moment she does this. The smell of their bed when she woke up every morning from beside him. That short time of her life felt a lot like love, a lot like the warmth of a place called home that a man sets up to be in till his end. Heera's nose quivers. The mixed smell of her used jasmine attar, Jalaal's long nights of closely kissing and making love while the children slept in other rooms over and under their cots, and then the smell of blood. His battered body, shot down by multiple bullets and drenched in blood, comes back to her. She hasn't forgotten the sight of waiting for him at the airport, his emerging to wave at her, and while walking towards her, being brought down by a rain of bullets. No one knows where they came from in police uniforms, but they were not the police. They were the enemies Heera and Jalaal had made by being at the top of their game and overlooking the well-being of each of their people.

Heera's breath is enflamed with rage. She looks away from the photograph with great difficulty. Her bed remains empty, and her nights end in a solemn desolation. Did she know they were going to end up like this? Did being the well-wisher of the large community and going against the rules and lines drawn by society and administration do a greater good? Is a man born destined for so much? Some people must have lives that are much more eventful than the number of years they have lived. Heera wipes her moist eyes and goes out into the thin, long verandah, knocking on the doors of each of her children. Its dawn, time to rise and start what a man does to run his home and work. Their work is now more difficult than ever before, with Sadanand, now a senior police officer, having brought up a mighty team that scans the docks and the airport like nobody's business. Today, a ship arrives loaded with gold and silver bars. This is a tough assignment, as there's another group of boys who, even a couple of years ago, worked under Rizwaan. Heera had tried so much to ask them to stick together and stay stronger. But the youngest of them all, Dilbar, refused her offer. He seemed a born leader; his mad eyes told Herera he could go over the edge and do anything to reach the top. An imaginary top in the heads of those who haven't been there. From where Heera sees reaching the top, there is a place full of responsibilities and more responsibilities.

By the time Heera has come back from her Namaaz and daily ablutions, Rizwaan's wife Najma has got tea and Paav ready for the full family. They sit on the floor and sip into the brown, fuming sweet tea. Heera bites into a paav, letting food into her system after last afternoon. She has been working away lately, counting money, allocating funds, and choosing assignments, often losing track of time while going for hours without food. These are her years of staying aware and awake. What her children can't foresee, she compensates for. As Rizwaan's little girl, Noor, crawls up to her grandmother's lap, she kisses the baby. Heera's scrutinising eyes are also looking for Haider. Of late, he has been missing work, drinking too much in town, and visiting brothels. An unshaven Haider comes late, while the others sip their tea as if they haven't noticed him. Heera asks for the plan. Rizwaan knows Dilbar will make an attempt to rescue the goods, win the confidence of the dark lord seated in distant lands, and thus bring Heera down. Rizwan tells Heera, drawing with his finger on the floor, how he, Haider, and Ashfaq will manage to protect the goods once they land. Panna, a young woman, now comes and hugs Heera from behind, planting a kiss on her Ammi's head. She dotingly comes and sits between her mother and sister-in-law, a warm blush of youth and probably love invading her. She is in love with Arun, one of the boys working under Rizwaan. Heera's heart trembles, thinking of a similar future as hers and Jalaal's for Panna. The trade is good to be of service and use to the community, but for continuity, Heera wouldn't marry Panna to a boy with a similar future as her own. In a deep, secret compartment of her mind, she is working on a plan with Najma to get the girl off the city for a few months and send her to Latur, where Najma's family lives spread over acres.

As all thoughts race in her mind at the same time, Heera looks over her entire family, and as sunlight invades their faces, they laugh and talk like there will be no tomorrow. Somewhere in the discussion of their work, in Ashfaq, she feels Jalaal, smiling away, doing a cheeky Salaam, and blowing her a kiss. She knows this is the only place called paradise. Their work and the things they do give them permission to only dream and enjoy this far. Tomorrow is a fantasy.

www.ingramcontent.com/pod-product-compliance
Lightning Source LLC
LaVergne TN
LVHW061559070526
838199LV00077B/7116